THE MISSING BOOKSHOP

Katie
Clapham

Kirsti
Beautyman

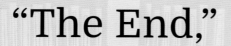

"The End,"

Mrs Minty said as she closed the book and smiled at the children on the rainbow carpet.

THE
MISSING
BOOKSHOP

For all my fellow indie booksellers — Katie

To Linda and Dave Drayton, my
mammar and pops, for instilling a love
of reading and books in me — Kirsti

STRIPES PUBLISHING LTD
An imprint of the Little Tiger Group
1 Coda Studios, 189 Munster Road, London SW6 6AW

First published in Great Britain in 2019

Text copyright © Katie Clapham, 2019
Illustrations copyright © Kirsti Beautyman, 2019

ISBN: 978-1-78895-042-8

The right of Katie Clapham and Kirsti Beautyman to be identified as
the author and illustrator of this work respectively has been asserted
by them in accordance with the Copyright, Designs and Patents Act, 1988.

Printed and bound in China.

STP/1800/0244/0419

2 4 6 8 10 9 7 5 3

"Thank you for coming to story time
and I hope to see you all next week."

1

Milly never missed
story time at Minty's
Bookshop. Mrs Minty
knew about every
book in the whole
world. Milly liked to
set her challenges.

"One with
a bear in!"

"One with
pirates!"

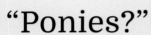

"Ponies?"

"Aliens!"

Mrs Minty always
had just the thing.

"So, Milly," said Mum, coming over. "Have you decided?"

Today was a special day because Milly had saved enough pocket money to buy a book.

4

"I think I'd like some sort of

sea adventure,"

Milly replied excitedly.

"Aha!" said Mrs Minty. "I have

just the thing!"

Mrs Minty got up from her creaky wooden story chair.

"Goodness! I'm getting a bit creaky, too!"
she said. She smiled but Milly couldn't help
noticing how slowly she walked.

Mrs Minty trailed her fingers along one of the
shelves and pulled out a book with a turquoise
cover and gold writing.

"I think you'll like this," she said,
her eyes twinkling. "It's full of mermaids
and sea monsters."

Milly took the book and opened it at the first page.

"Hang on, Milly,"
Mum called.

"We need to pay for it first! Why don't you tidy up the story area while I find your pocket money for Mrs Minty?"

Milly handed her mum the book and went to
collect up the colourful cushions.

The colours didn't look that bright any more.

She turned one over to see if the other side looked
better but that was all worn, too.

Looking round the bookshop she
could see the paint was starting to
peel off round the window frames
and the curtains were faded.

9

But it still looked sort of marvellous
because it was filled with
shelves and **shelves**

of wonderful
books.

Milly glanced over at the picture
of Mrs Minty and her daughter
sitting on the wooden story chair
when it was brand new.

Mrs Minty looked quite different now.

In the picture, Mrs Minty didn't
have her little reading glasses
and her long silver hair was as
red as an apple.

"Time to go, Milly,"
her mum called.

As Milly left the bookshop, a little worry cloud formed above her head.

Mrs Minty, her wooden story chair and her whole bookshop were all getting a bit creaky.

Milly and her mum always popped into the café after story time. But today Milly couldn't concentrate on her new book. Or her strawberry smoothie.

"What do you do if something is old and creaky?" she asked her mum.

"Well you have to treat it very carefully, so it doesn't break. But eventually it might need replacing with something new," Milly's mum said, sipping her tea.

Milly was shocked.

Mrs Minty couldn't be replaced!

That night Minty looked at her bookshelves. They were filled with books from Minty's Bookshop: funny stories of children making mischief, exotic tales of old kings, amazing atlases, picture books and books of poems. Mrs Minty had helped her choose every one.

The bookshop could never close!
Milly snuggled under her duvet. Perhaps if everyone
looked after it, it wouldn't break and it wouldn't need
to be replaced. As she fell asleep, Milly thought
about all the things she could do to help.

At story time the following week, Milly was extra helpful.

She chose the
comfiest cushion
for Mrs Minty's
story chair...

She laid out
the cushions for the
other children...

...and she tidied them all away at the end.

She even helped one boy find a copy of the book Mrs Minty had been reading from.

"You'd make a wonderful
bookseller, Milly!"
Mrs Minty joked.

But was it a joke? Milly couldn't help wondering.

Did Mrs Minty
want her to run the
bookshop?

Milly thought working in a
bookshop might be the best
grown-up job there could be
but she wasn't a grown-up yet!

Milly watched Mrs Minty helping a customer.

"I'm looking for a book for my nephew. He plays cricket," a lady was saying.

"We've got lots of books about cricket," said Mrs Minty.

"And a book for my niece – she's just got a pet bearded dragon!"

"I'll have to order it in, but I know just the thing."

Mrs Minty was a walking
encyclopedia when it came to
books. How could Milly ever
learn to be like that?

As Milly followed Mum up
the road, her worry cloud
grew a little heavier.

Minty's Bookshop was
truly irreplaceable.

At the café, Milly had another question for Mum.

"If Mrs Minty couldn't run the bookshop any more, would it just close down?"

"That would be up to Mrs Minty," said Mum. "She could look for someone to take over, but if not she might have to sell the shop and it could get turned into something else."

Milly gasped. If nobody else wanted to run Minty's it might be replaced with a bank or an opticians.

What use were glasses
if there were no books to read?

If Mrs Minty could just stay until Milly
was grown-up and had become an
encyclopaedia of books...

Milly leaped to her feet.

"Can we go back to
the bookshop, Mum?
There's something
I need to tell
Mrs Minty."

Milly's mum waited outside while Milly
raced back inside the shop.

"Mrs Minty!" she called out.
"Mrs Minty!"

ANTONIO'S

BANK

23

"I just needed to tell you
that ... banks are very boring and
bookshops are very important.
I love your shop. I love coming to story
time but I want to sit on the rainbow carpet
and **not on the wooden story chair.**
I'd **love** to work here one day but
I'm not an encyclopaedia yet and
**Minty's Bookshop can
never be replaced!"**

It all came out so fast and jumbled up. Mrs Minty looked rather surprised.

"Well, Milly, thank you. I think I agree with everything you said." She smiled. "If you keep coming to story time, I'll keep telling the stories. How's that?"

"Just the thing," Milly said and they both laughed.

Milly's worry cloud almost disappeared over the weekend. After school on Monday they headed to the bookshop as usual.

But the
bookshop
was
closed.

"That's odd! I'm sure Mrs Minty would've told us if she was going away," Mum said as Milly peered through the locked door. There was no sign of Mrs Minty and no notice on the door to say when she'd be back.

"I hope she's all right!" Mum said. But even she looked worried. "How about a smoothie?" she suggested.

But Milly shook her head. There was no way she could enjoy a smoothie today.

They checked
the shop
after school
every day.

The following
week there
was a sign
that said...

CLOSED
DUE TO
UNFORESEEN
CIRCUMSTANCES

...which Milly's mum said meant that something had happened that no one had planned.

The week after that, it said...

CLOSED
UNTIL
FURTHER
NOTICE

...which meant that
no one knew when it
would be open again.

The week after that, Milly and her mum found a van outside the shop. It was filled with things from the bookshop. The rainbow carpet was rolled up. The faded cushions were piled on top of each other.

The dusty picture frames were lying in a heap. And Mrs Minty's wooden story chair was upside down on top of a cardboard box.

A tall lady with her hair tied up in a spotty scarf came out of the bookshop and closed the van door.

She got into the driver's cab and drove away before Milly had a chance to say anything.

Mum took Milly's
hand and they walked
up to the café.

But even a slice of
Victoria sponge couldn't
help Milly shake the sad
feeling in her tummy.

Mrs Minty had
gone and it looked
like her bookshop
was going to be
replaced.

The next time they saw it, the
bookshop was boarded up and
the sign said 'For Sale'.
Milly's mum said that meant
things were going to change.

FOR
SALE
CALL: 0020412

It was a wet weekend. Milly usually loved wet weekends. It meant she could sit on her window seat reading without Mum telling her to go outside.

But today the words seemed to swim in front of her eyes.

Mum came in with a mug of hot chocolate. "What are you reading, Milly?"

Milly showed her the cover. It was a story about a girl who loved books and it was one of her all-time favourites.

"*Matilda*!" Her mum smiled. "Haven't you read that one a million times?"

"Yes but it makes me feel better when I feel sad."

"Oh dear. Is it because of Mrs Minty?" Mum asked, sitting down next to her.

Milly closed the book and
snuggled into her mum.

"I can't stop thinking about her! Where has
she gone? Why is the shop closed? Who is
changing it and what will they change it to?"

"Oh Milly, these are all good questions but I
don't have the answers I'm afraid."

Milly could feel tears in her eyes. "Do you
think Minty's could be replaced by
another bookshop?"

"I hope so, Milly," her mum said, picking up
Matilda. "Now, where did you get to?"
They took it in turns reading the last few chapters.
Matilda had a very happy ending, it always did.

"Try not to worry, Milly," her mum said
as she tucked her into bed that night.
"We'll find out what happened to
Mrs Minty, I promise."

Milly tried to fall asleep. She tried to think of nice places where Mrs Minty could be.

Maybe she was reading a book on a deserted island...

Or sitting by a lake...

Or sipping a coffee in a busy city...

But why would she suddenly go away
without telling anyone?

By Sunday afternoon Milly had come up with a plan. Wherever Mrs Minty was, it was up to Milly to find someone to run the bookshop for her. Someone who loved books. Someone who knew how much the town needed a bookshop. Someone who could see Minty's the way she saw it... And she knew just what to do.

She fetched her crayons and began to draw the bookshop – not as it looked today but as she imagined it looked when it first opened.

With bright yellow paintwork, flowers in the window boxes and a beautiful window display. The red door was wide open showing a hint of the books inside. It looked amazing.

On the way home from school on **Monday**,
Milly asked her mum to help her stick her picture to
the boarded-up bookshop.

"It's a wonderful picture, Milly," said
Mum. "I know Mrs Minty would love it."

Milly smiled. Mrs Minty would love it
but Milly needed whoever was going to
buy the shop to love it, too.

On **Tuesday**, there was another picture stuck to the boards next to Milly's.

It was a drawing of Mrs Minty on her wooden story chair.

On **Wednesday**, someone had added a note. It said:

On **Thursday**, there
was a poem. Milly's
mum read it out to her.

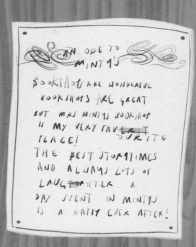

It was called **'An Ode to Minty's'**,
which she said meant it was all about how
much the writer loved the bookshop.

On **Friday**, there were too many
new things to count. Drawings,
letters and photographs were stuck
all round Milly's picture.

There was no way the new owners
could ignore this.

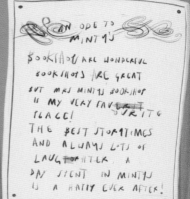

AN ODE TO
MINTYS

BOOKSHOPS ARE WONDERFUL
BOOKSHOPS ARE GREAT
BUT MRS MINTYS BOOKSHOP
IS MY VERY FAVOURITE
PLACE!
THE BEST STORYTIMES
AND ALWAYS LOTS OF
LAUGHTER. A
DAY SPENT IN MINTYS
IS A HAPPY EVER AFTER!

SAVE
OUR
BOOK
SHOP

The weekend brought warm sunshine. Milly was sitting in her neighbour's garden while her mum was at the supermarket.

She was reading about the Egyptians when her mum came rushing through the back door still carrying the shopping.

"Milly! There's a new sign at the bookshop! And guess what? It says a new bookshop will be opening in one week!"

It was a long week.

Every time Milly and her mum passed the bookshop Milly couldn't help peeping through the gaps in the boards.

More notes and pictures had been added.

Someone had started a countdown.

63

The night before
the grand opening,
Milly could
hardly sleep.

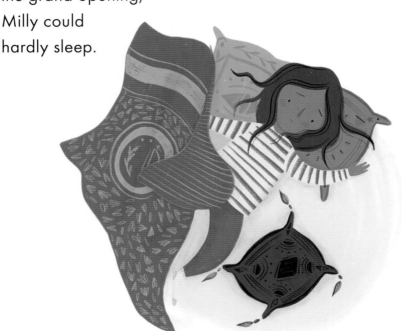

She couldn't wait
to visit the new
bookshop.

But she couldn't stop thinking about Mrs Minty, too.

What had happened to her?

And could Milly learn to love the new owners of the bookshop?

On Saturday morning, Milly danced by the front door, desperate to get going.

"There's no need to race," her mum laughed as they set off. "It's open all day!"

As the bookshop came into view, Milly couldn't believe her eyes.

It looked exactly like her drawing!

The paintwork was the same sunflower yellow.
The window boxes were filled with flowers.
There were balloons and bunting in among the
window displays. And through the open door she
could see shelves and shelves of books.

"Welcome to Minty's Bookshop!"

It was the lady with the spotty head scarf!

"It's still Minty's!" Milly couldn't help shouting out.
Mum squeezed her hand.

"It sure is. Allow me to introduce myself –
I'm Mo Minty. I'm Mrs Minty's daughter."

Milly was a little confused. Mo Minty was the
little girl in the photograph. How could she be
the tall lady in the spotty headscarf?

"But you're all grown up!" Milly said.

"Well, I am on the outside but I still love children's books – in fact my favourite book of all time is *Matilda*. Have you read it?"

"I love *Matilda*!" Milly grinned, already certain that she could learn to love Mo Minty.

"But wait... Where is Mrs Minty?" Milly asked.

"She's right over there."

Milly spun round and there was Mrs Minty, sitting in her newly painted wooden chair, ready to begin story time.

Milly's worry cloud burst open and a happy feeling rained down over her.

Mrs Minty and her bookshop were back.

She ran through the bookshop and threw her arms round Mrs Minty.

"I've been so worried about you,"
she said.

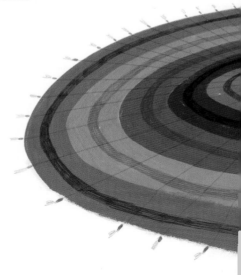

"Oh Milly, I am sorry," said Mrs Minty, "I had a fall and I went to stay with Mo while I got better. Mo wanted me to move in with her. She even came back here to collect my things and put the shop up for sale."

Mo took over the story. "But then something amazing happened. I came over to tidy the shop after we'd packed everything up and I saw the picture...

"It was a beautiful drawing of the bookshop just as I remembered it when I was little. I knew how special it was to me and suddenly the thought of it closing made me very sad."

"But that was MY drawing!" cried Milly.

Mrs Minty chuckled. "I had a feeling it was. So now Mo's moving here instead to run the bookshop."

"With Mum's help of course. No one knows more about books than her!" added Mo.

"She's an encyclopedia of books," Milly agreed.

"Are you talking about my mummy?" a little girl in a spotty dress said.

"No, Tilly, we're talking about Granny!" said Mo.

"Well, you know a lot about books, too, Mummy," said Tilly. "And so do I," she added.

Mo laughed. "Milly, this is my daughter Tilly – short for Matilda."

"Milly knows a lot about books, too," said Mrs Minty. "She never misses a story time."

"Do you want to sit next to me?" Tilly said, reaching out and holding Milly's hand.

"One day I'll run the bookshop, but I'm too little now. You could help me if you like."

"Milly and Tilly's Bookshop! I like the sound of that!" Mo laughed.

"Maybe after story time with Granny, you girls could draw a picture of your own bookshop for our wall..."

Mo pointed to a brand-new display on the wall.
It was all of the notes, photos, poems and letters
that had been stuck to the builders' boards,
each in their own coloured frame.

And in the very centre, in a big sunflower-yellow wooden frame, was Milly's drawing.

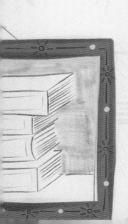

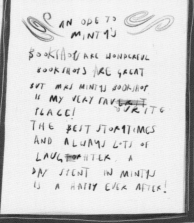